This book belongs to

_____

Avengers, Assemble!

The greatest super heroes in the world are gathered in this book to defend the galaxy from evil, and they need your help! Within these pages, you'll hone your crime-fighting skills by decoding messages from Nick Fury, solving mazes and puzzles featuring your favorite champions, and coloring in the coolest Avenger symbols meant for your eyes only.

But that's not all!

There are also **three** action-packed comics for you to finish with stickers and stencils any way you like! Can Thor, Falcon, and Ant-Man take on Thanos? What secrets await Iron Man, Doctor Strange, and Captain America at the far reaches of the globe? And in a competition between Black Panther, Hulk, and Black Widow, who would emerge victorious?

Suit up and get ready. It's time to turn the page and prove you've got what it takes to become an Avenger!

Thanos' Revenge!

It's a quiet day in New York City . . . until the Avengers get an emergency call from Nick Fury!

Falcon, Thor, and Ant-Man swoop in to take down the Mad Titan. But Thanos has a terrible plan.

Use your stencils to add word balloons and sound effects to this story!

Thanos is about to use his Infinity Gauntlet to destroy the city! Can Falcon, Thor, and Ant-Man stop him in time?

Use your stickers to create their final battle, and add word balloons, captions, and sound effects!

Hidden Heroes

The Avengers' names are hidden in the word search below.
Search up, down, across, and diagonally to find and circle them.

**THOR · IRON MAN · BLACK WIDOW · BLACK PANTHER ·
HULK · VISION · ANT-MAN · CAPTAIN AMERICA · HAWKEYE**

```
C A P T A I N A M E R I C A
F N C H O Q R Z M Y D P E H
J T B O V C O O L A U Z X P
I M L R B A E E N J W X P Q
N A A R V A S D F M G H J K
P N C O I U N T R E A W Q A
S D K F G A H J H K L N M N
V B P V Z C X Z U A S R F T
I D A T Z U U L L N Y A S D
S F N G B L A C K W I D O W
I A T Q W E R T Y U I O P L
O K H J H G F D S A Z X C V
N B E N M N H A W K E Y E U
Y T R R E W S D F V H D B L
```

Suit Up

Captain America is missing some important pieces of his uniform. Connect the dots to reveal the missing items below. Then color the picture.

Tic-Tac-Target

Hawkeye never misses his mark! Can you make your mark in these games of tic-tac-toe? Challenge a friend to see who can win the most rounds!

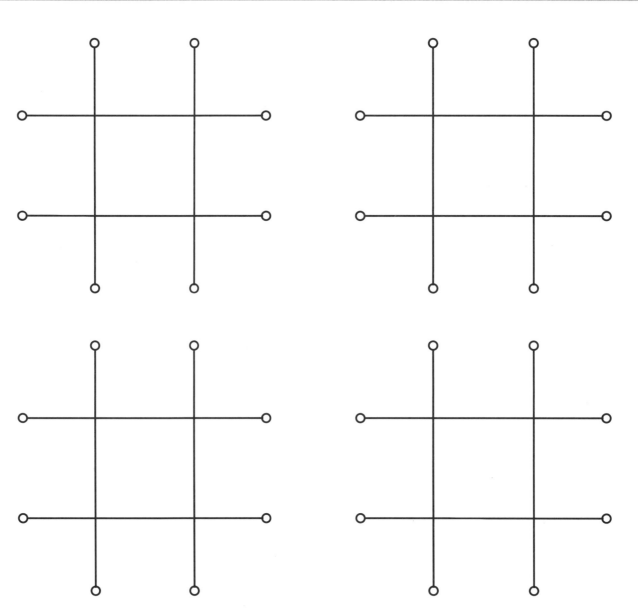

The Armed Avenger

Use the key below to color in Iron Man's symbol.

1 = Red
2 = Yellow
3 = Blue
4 = Black

Tell the Tale

The Avengers are on an interstellar mission in space. But they've been attacked by an unknown enemy! Use the space on these two pages to write how you think the story goes.

_____

_____

_____

_____

_____

_____

_____

_____

_____

_____

Icy Peril

At the far reaches of the globe, three unlikely figures emerge from a portal. It's Doctor Strange, Iron Man, and Captain America!

My mystic portal was able to bring us here, Tony. But are you **sure** this is the location of the distress signal?

The Avengers find an abandoned research facility in the glacier. Someone is waiting for them!

Red Skull has brainwashed Bucky, and now the Winter Soldier is going to fight the Avengers! Can the heroes stop him in time?

Use your stencils to add word balloons and sound effects to this story!

This is the Avengers' last chance to free Bucky from Red Skull's power!

Use your stickers to determine the Winter Soldier's fate, and add word balloons, captions, and sound effects!

Double Vision

Unscramble the words below to reveal the Avengers' names.

LKCAB DIWOW _____ _____

ISVINO _____

GCOERO TDSANTR _____ _____

SPAW _____

NAM-TAN _____ - _____

YEWKEAH _____

LNOAFC _____

HCN ARWEIMA _____ _____

LOKi
Master of Mischief

Loki is the God of Mischief!
Color this picture to show the
maniacal magician is up to no good.

Brother vs. Brother

Thor and Loki are battling on Asgard!

Play Dots and Boxes with a friend to determine who will win in the showdown and find the most Cosmic Cubes. Have one player choose *T* for Thor, and the other *L* for Loki. Take turns drawing one horizontal or vertical line between the dots. If your line completes a box, write your *T* or *L* initial in the center, then go again. The player with the most completed boxes (Cosmic Cubes) at the end wins.

Mystic Numbers

Doctor Strange is opening a magic portal. Solve the math problems below, then use the code to find out what special object he needs to complete his spell.

10 - 8 =	6 + 9 =	40 - 7 =	12 ÷ 2 =	11 x 3 =	4 x 5 =	14 - 1 =	56 ÷ 7 =	1 +11 =

___ ___   ___ ___ ___ ___ ___ ___

CODE:

15	8	12	2	20	33	11	6	0	13
A	N	G	W	T	S	K	P	Q	I

Infinity Stones

There are six Infinity Stones. Unscramble the words below to reveal the names of each. Then write them on the lines and color the picture.

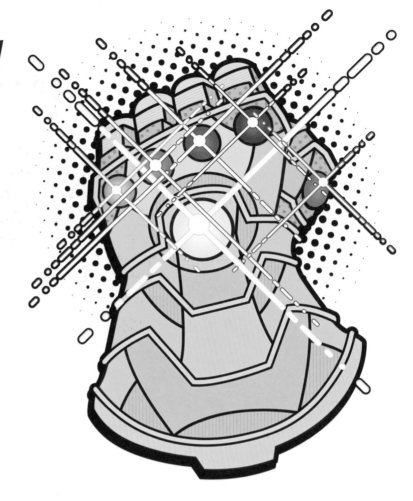

WPROE _____

NDIM _____

LUOS _____

ATREILY _____

EPASC _____

MITE _____

Earth's Mightiest Heroes

The Avengers are the strongest heroes on Earth! Color the picture below to show their might.

Spot the Differences

There are six differences between the two images below.
Find and circle them.

Competition of Champions

The Avengers always work together as a team to defend the galaxy from evil.

But sometimes, they like to practice to make sure their fighting skills are at peak performance!

What do you say, Hulk? Which one of us is quicker?

Hulk say . . . Hulk SMASH!

Now, boys, play nice. After all, if there's a master of stealth and speed, I think we can all agree it's *me*.

Black Panther, Hulk, and Black Widow are testing their skills at the Avengers' headquarters! Use your stencils to add word balloons and sound effects to this story.

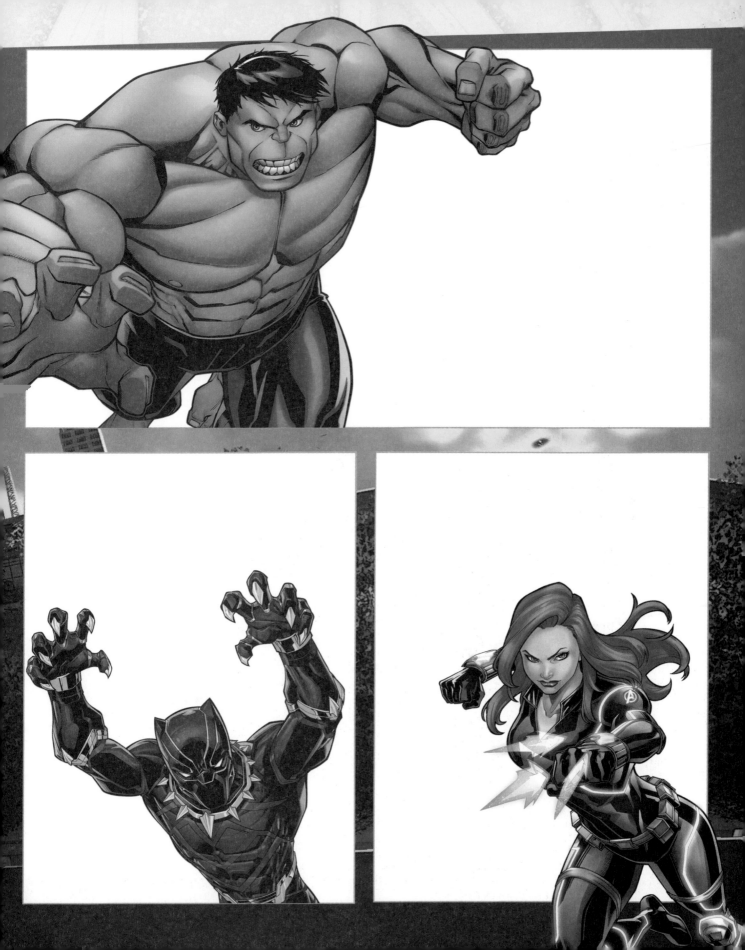

Who will win the friendly sparring match and earn the title *Quickest Avenger?*

Use your stickers to complete the competition, and add word balloons, captions, and sound effects!

Hero at Heart

Do you think you have what it takes to be an Avenger?
Use the space below to draw yourself as a super hero.
Use your stencils to add word balloons and sound effects, too!

Weapon Wordplay

The names of seven Avenger weapons are hidden in the word search below. Search up, down, across, and diagonally to find and circle them.

HAMMER • SHIELD • SLING RING • BOW AND ARROW • FISTS • LASER BLASTERS • ANT-MAN SUIT

```
Q W E R T Y U I O P L B K J
H S L I N G R I N G G O F D
S D F G H J K L M N B W V C
X Z A W D R A F T H U A S U
P L O K I J N U N H B N H X
D V G B H N T K M I J D I Y
Z F A D H A M M E R C A E Q
A W I S R F A Y G U N R L G
V C T S V R N X E A T R D V
Z Q R V T A S T V E N O I D
E B U Z X S U T G I N W Q M
O H Y H S B I I W B L S X Y
Z X R V J O T S W Q A I J N
L A S E R B L A S T E R S Z
```

Power Supreme

Connect the dots to reveal the only item that can wield the power of all six Infinity Stones.

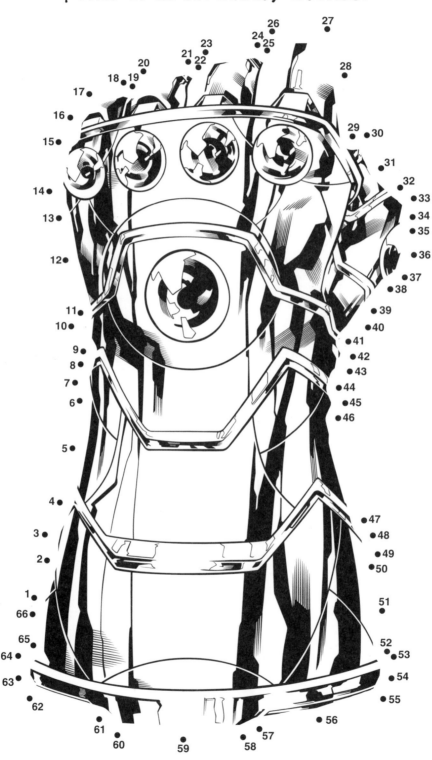

Computer Virus

Ultron has taken over Tony Stark's computer system and has locked out each system using the name of a different Avenger enemy as the password! Help Tony regain command by unscrambling the villainous names below.

SONHAT _____

DEK URLLS _____ _____

YHRAD _____

IOKL _____

EKRE _____

JELLOTAKCYEW _____

Comic of Heroes!

Use these panels to draw your own super hero comic! Include drawings of the Avengers, of yourself as a super hero, or even made-up champions of justice. Use your stencils to add word balloons and sound effects, too.

Hawk-Eyes

Can you spot the following things hidden in this image?

- 7 stars
- 4 diamonds
- 3 arrows
- 2 hammers
- 1 Avengers symbol
- 1 Black Panther symbol

Answer Key

Page 12:

```
C A P T A I N A M E R I C A
F N C H O Q R Z M Y D P E H
J T B O V C C O L A U Z X P
I M L R B A E E N J W X P Q
N A A R V A S D F M G H J A
P N C O I U N T R E A W Q A
S D K F G A H J H K L N M N
V B P V Z C X Z U A S R F T
I D A T Z U U L L N Y A S D
S F N G B L A C K W I D O W
I A T Q W E R T Y U I O P L
O K H J H G F D S A Z X C V
N B E N M N H A W K E Y E U
Y T R R E W S D F V H D B L
```

Page 26:

BLACK   WIDOW

VISION

DOCTOR   STRANGE

WASP

ANT _ MAN

HAWKEYE

FALCON

WAR   MACHINE

Page 29:

W A S P   S T I N G

Page 30:

POWER

MIND

SOUL

REALITY

SPACE

TIME

Pages 32-33:

Page 41:

```
Q W E R T Y U I O P L B K J
H S L I N G R I N G G O F D
S D F G H J K L M N B W V C
X Z A W D R A F T H U A S U
P L O K I J N U N H B N H X
D V G B H N T K M I J D I Y
Z F A D H A M M E R C A E Q
A W I S R F A Y G U N T L G
V C T S R N X E A T R R V
Z Q R V T A S T V E N O I D
E B U Z X S U T G I N W Q M
O H Y H S B I I W B L S X Y
Z X R V J O T S W Q A I J N
L A S E R B L A S T E R S Z
```

Page 43:

THANOS

RED   SKULL

HYDRA

LOKI

KREE

YELLOWJACKET

Page 46:

Stickers for pages 24-25

Stickers for pages 38-39

© 2021 MARVEL